A BIG CHEESE
FOR THE WHITE HOUSE

The True Tale of a Tremendous Cheddar

by Candace Fleming

illustrated by S. D. Schindler

SQUARE FISH

FARRAR STRAUS GIROUX
NEW YORK

For Melanie Kroupa, editor extraordinaire — C.F.

A NOTE ABOUT THE TEXT

While all the events in this story are true, it must be noted that some of the characters are not. Goodwife Todgers, Farmer Fuzzlewit, Farmer Durdles, little Humphrey Crock, and Phineas Dobbs are all figments of my imagination. Also, I have chosen to use the phrase "White House" as it is more familiar to today's readers, even though the structure was commonly known as the President's House until about 1809.

SQUARE FISH

An Imprint of Macmillan

A BIG CHEESE FOR THE WHITE HOUSE.
Text copyright © 1999 by Candace Fleming.
Illustrations copyright © 1999 by S. D. Schindler.
All rights reserved. Printed in China by South China Printing Company Ltd.,
Dongguan City, Guangdong Province. For information, address
Square Fish, 175 Fifth Avenue, New York, NY 10010.

Square Fish and the Square Fish logo are trademarks of Macmillan and
are used by Farrar Straus Giroux under license from Macmillan.

Library of Congress Cataloging-in-Publication Data
Fleming, Candace.
    A big cheese for the White House : the true tale of a tremendous
cheddar / Candace Fleming ; illustrated by S. D Schindler.
        p.   cm.
    Summary: In 1801, the townspeople of Cheshire, Massachusetts,
create a gigantic cheddar cheese to present to President Jefferson
at his New Year's Day party.
    ISBN 978-0-374-40627-1
    [1. Cheese—Fiction. 2. Cheshire (Mass.)—History—19th
century—Fiction. 3. Jefferson, Thomas, 1743-1826—Fiction.]
I. Schindler, S. D., ill. II. Title.
PZ7.F59936Bi 2004   [E]—dc21   2003048058

Originally published in the United States by Farrar Straus Giroux
First Square Fish Edition: June 2012
Square Fish logo designed by Filomena Tuosto
mackids.com

10 9 8 7 6

AR: 4.1 / LEXILE: AD450L

CHESHIRE, MASSACHUSETTS, made mouthwatering cheese.

Wheels of cheese. Chunks of cheese. Wedges of cheese. Hunks of cheese.

So lovingly processed and perfectly aged was Cheshire's cheese that people from Philadelphia to Boston bought it by the boatload.

"Yessiree," the villagers of Cheshire often boasted. "It's Cheshire cheese, the best you can serve at your table."

But one July evening, the villagers heard news that threatened to sour their curds forever.

"I hear folks in Norton, Connecticut, are coloring their cheddar green and blue," reported Farmer Fuzzlewit at the Cheshire town meeting.

"And I hear they're adding flavors like cranberry and molasses to their curds," added Farmer Durdles.

"That's not the worst of it," moaned Goodwife Todgers. And then she spoke the words that caused an uproar among her fellow citizens. "I hear President Thomas Jefferson himself is serving Norton cheese in the nation's capital."

In the midst of this commotion, Elder John Leland strode to the front of the room.

"Folks," he shouted, "I have an idea. A very large idea. If each of you will give one day's milking from each of your many cows, we can put our curds together and create a whopping big cheddar."

"But what will we do with it?" asked little Humphrey Crock.

"We'll give it to President Jefferson, of course," exclaimed Elder John.

Goodwife Todgers clapped her hands. "With a cheese that size, the President will be serving it for years. And that means he won't be serving Norton cheese."

A loud snort came from the back of the room. "Ridiculous," scoffed Phineas Dobbs. "It can't be done."

The next morning, before the roosters crowed, the great cheddar adventure got under way.

Wagon after wagon rattled into the town square. Each delivered a steady stream of milk — milk that swelled into a cow-created river.

"By Jupiter!" exclaimed Elder John, emptying his own buckets into the brimming troughs. "This must be the work of hundreds of cows."

"Nine hundred and thirty-four," said little Humphrey Crock, who was good at arithmetic.

With the milking done, everyone gathered before the town hall.

The men warmed the milk and told jokes.

The women broke the curds and sang songs.

The children giggled and sprinkled the salt.

At last it was time to press.

"I don't suppose any of you have noticed that the cheese press isn't big enough to handle all those curds," Phineas said.

Elder John and the others looked from the mountain of curds to the tiny cheese press.

"Could we squeeze them with our bare hands?" asked Farmer Fuzzlewit.

"Or stomp on them with our bare feet?" suggested Goodwife Todgers.

Phineas snorted. "I told you before. It can't be done."

But Farmer Durdles jumped up. "Oh, yes, it can! Our cheese press may be small, but our apple press isn't."

"You're right!" exclaimed Elder John. "Why, if that press can smash an orchardful of apples, it can surely handle these curds!"

And with the help of the village men, he set about dragging the huge press into the square.

Squish-thump! went the press as it squeezed the watery whey from the curds. *Squish-thump! Squish-thump! Squish-thump!*

All afternoon the curds were fed into the press. But just before nightfall, Phineas pointed out a whole new problem. "There's not a hoop made that can hold all that cheese."

For once the villagers were silent.

"I told you it couldn't be done," Phineas said.

Just then John Cribbs, the village blacksmith, stood. "Wait! I can make us a hoop!" he hollered. "I'll make one right now!"

"Hallelujah!" cried Elder John. And he manned the bellows as the blacksmith pounded out a

BIG . . .

"Ooh!" squealed Goodwife Todgers.

. . . BIGGER . . .

"Aah!" gasped little Humphrey Crock.

. . . the BIGGEST cheese hoop the good citizens of Cheshire had ever seen.

"Hmmph!" grumbled Phineas.

Quickly, the villagers lined it with cloth and packed the newly pressed cheese inside. It was dark when the day's work was hoisted onto the huge cattle scale.

"Ladies and gentlemen," Elder John announced, "our efforts have produced a true cheesemaking miracle. This cheddar tips the scales at one thousand two hundred and thirty-five pounds and stands four feet high! Why, it's taller than Humphrey Crock!"

The men whooped and hollered and kissed their wives.

The women clapped and cheered and grinned ear-to-ear.

The children turned cartwheels and danced in the street.

Only Phineas stood unmoving, his arms across his chest.

The others ignored him. Heaving the big cheese into a wagon, they hauled it to Elder John's barn to age and ripen . . .

    and ripen . . .

        and ripen . . .

as month after month went by.

The villagers took turns checking their cheese. Every day they turned it to keep it from cracking and tasted a morsel to test its flavor.

Finally, one cold November morning, Goodwife Todgers announced, "Perfect in taste and texture. It's Cheshire cheese, the best you can serve at your table."

"Hmmph!" Phineas Dobbs sniffed. "You still have to get it to President Jefferson, and I say it can't be done."

"But I say it can," said Elder John. "I'll take our cheese to Washington, D.C., and give it to the President as a New Year's Day gift from the town of Cheshire — the country's biggest cheese for the nation's greatest man."

"Hmmph . . . a fool's errand," argued Phineas. "There's no way you can get that cheese across the country all by yourself."

"You're right, Phineas," agreed Elder John. "That's exactly why *you're* coming with me."

The very next morning, the villagers lugged the cheese from the barn and heaved it into Elder John's sleigh.

The horses bucked and kicked. The sleigh tipped.

And Phineas snorted, "Hmmph! I told you so. It can't be done."

But Elder John hitched another horse to the sleigh. Then, with a crack of the whip, he waved farewell.

For two whole days Elder John, the giant cheese, and a doubting
Phineas sledded over the snow-packed roads.

Finally they arrived in Hudson, New York.

The ship's crew loaded the cheese on deck. Then down the Hudson River sailed man and cheddar.

News of the cheese traveled faster than the ship. At every port, people flocked to catch a glimpse.

"It's tremendous!" they cried. "It's stupendous! It's colossal! Gigantic! Mammoth!"

"It's Cheshire cheese," Elder John proudly replied. "The best you can serve at your table."

At last the ship docked in New York City. Elder John, Phineas, and the cheese debarked and began the last leg of their journey.

Traveling in a sleigh drawn by six white horses, the cheese was a spectacular sight.

By the time the cheese-laden sleigh rattled into Washington, its citizens were waiting.

"It's the mammoth cheese!" people shouted, racing from their shops, their schools, and houses.

Trumpets sounded. Banners waved. The Army band played.

Elder John and Phineas made their way straight to the White House and President Jefferson's New Year's Day party.

When the sleigh halted before the mansion's front door, Phineas loudly harrumphed. "You think a fine man like President Jefferson is going to let two cheesemongers and a big cheddar into his fancy party?"

Just then, the front door swung open.

"It's the big cheese!" cried the doorman. "The President has been expecting you!"

Fifteen footmen heaved the cheese from the sleigh.

Elder John and Phineas trotted nervously behind.

They bowed to President Jefferson and his glittering guests.

With a *THUMP!* the footmen dropped the cheese before the President.

President Jefferson was speechless. Never had he seen such a cheese.

Elder John cleared his throat. "As representative of the people of Cheshire, Massachusetts," he said, "I present this cheese as a New Year's Day gift."

"I will cause this event to be placed in the records of our nation," President Jefferson announced. "And it will ever shine amidst its archives." Then he cut into the cheddar's golden glory.

The guests pushed forward, eager for a taste.

For the very first time since the plan was proposed, Phineas didn't snort. Instead he grinned.

"It's Cheshire cheese," he said proudly. "The best you can serve at your table."

A FINAL WORD ABOUT THOSE CURDS

THE BIG CHEESE remained in the nation's capital long after Elder John returned to Cheshire. Left standing in the East Room of the White House, the cheese was nibbled by the many guests who visited President Jefferson. Almost everyone who sampled the cheese claimed it was superb.

Sadly, by the next New Year's Day, sixty pounds of the cheese had to be removed from its middle because of decay. The remaining portion continued to grace the White House table. It was even served at a reception in honor of the Louisiana Purchase in 1803.

One source says the big cheese lasted until a presidential reception in 1805, where it was served with hot punch and cake. Another rumor has it that whatever was left of the cheese by that time was dumped into the Potomac River. One fact is clear, though. While President Jefferson remained in office, he never needed to serve Norton cheese at his table again.

As for the people of Cheshire?

They never forgot their big cheese. In 1940, they erected a concrete replica of it and the apple press. On the bronze plaque they engraved a likeness of Elder John Leland along with these words:

ELDER JOHN LELAND 1754–1841

THE BIG CHESHIRE CHEESE

WEIGHING 1235 LBS.